D0374377

THE GOOEY CHEWY CONTEST

by HOWARD GOLDSMITH
Illustrated by CHARLES JORDAN

MONDO

For Michelle, with affection—H.G.
For Charlie and Maggie—C.J.

Text copyright © 1997 by Howard Goldsmith
Illustrations copyright © 1997 by Mondo Publishing

All rights reserved.
No part of this publication may be reproduced, except in the
case of quotation for articles or reviews, or stored in any
retrieval system, or transmitted in any form or by any means,
electronic, mechanical, photocopying, recording, or otherwise,
without written permission from the publisher.

For information contact:
MONDO Publishing
980 Avenue of the Americas
New York, NY 10018
Visit our web site at http://www.mondopub.com

Designed by Mina Greenstein

Printed in Hong Kong by South China Printing Co. (1988) Ltd.
04 05 06 07   9 8 7 6

Library of Congress Cataloging-in-Publication Data
Goldsmith, Howard.
  The gooey chewy contest / by Howard Goldsmith ;
illustrated by Charles Jordan.
    p. cm.
  Summary: Tired of being ridiculed for his short stature by
the tallest boy in the class, Gabi decides to challenge him in
a bubble gum-blowing contest.
  ISBN 1-57255-221-2 (pbk. : alk. paper)
  [1. Size—Fiction. 2. Contests—Fiction. 3. Hispanic
Americans—Fiction.] I. Jordan, Charles, ill. II. Title.
PZ7.G575Go 1996
[E]—dc20
           96-15260
            CIP
            AC

Contents

The Contest

On his way home from school, Gabi passed a sign.

"I'm going to enter that bubble-blowing contest," Gabi told Joselito.

Joselito laughed. "A little kid like you? You know I blow the biggest bubbles in town."

Gabi Gomero was the shortest boy in his class. Joselito Flaquito was the tallest. Joselito always made fun of Gabi's height.

I'll show him what a little kid can do! thought Gabi. But he wondered how he could win the contest. Then he remembered Uncle Teo Cerebrito, the inventor. *I'll go ask Uncle Teo*, Gabi decided. *Maybe he can help me.*

Uncle Teo lived in Cerebrito Manor, a house he had built himself.

There was something special about
Cerebrito Manor. It looked like a space
ship. Gabi was always afraid Cerebrito
Manor might blast off into space, taking
Uncle Teo with it.

But the last time Gabi visited Uncle
Teo, the Manor was still there. Gabi
looked forward to seeing his uncle again.

The Bubble-Making Machine

When Gabi arrived at Cerebrito Manor, Uncle Teo shouted a warm greeting. "How are you, Gabi?"

Gabi told Uncle Teo about the bubble-blowing contest.

"Did you say bubble?" Uncle Teo exclaimed. "Come, I'll show you something." He led Gabi down the hall to a room at the rear of the house.

A large machine stood before them. "See if you can guess what this is," said Uncle Teo. "It's the only one of its kind in the entire world. That's because I made it!"

Gabi scratched his head, puzzled.

"I'll show you how it works," said Uncle Teo. He poured a bottle of liquid soap into an opening. Then he turned a crank. The machine shook up, down, sideways. CLANK! GURGLE! BOING! POW!

A large round bubble floated up out of the machine.

"Do you see that?" asked Uncle Teo. "A real beauty!"

Gabi tried to catch the bubble, but it flew up to the ceiling.

Another bubble rose from the machine, followed by a third, a fourth, and more. They went sailing by, too fast for Gabi to count.

"I get it," said Gabi. "It's a bubble-making machine."

"Correct!" Uncle Teo jumped up and down with glee. "Look at 'em go, boy!"

Bubbles streamed through the air, as thick as snowflakes during a storm.

"How do you turn it off?" Gabi asked.

Uncle Teo pressed a switch, but nothing happened. "The switch must be broken," he said, blowing a bubble off his nose.

The room was so filled with bubbles,
they kept bursting as they bounced off
the walls and ceiling. The machine
rocked back and forth, going BLOOP-
BLEEP, BLEEP-BLOP. Bubbles poured
out in endless numbers, faster and faster.

Finally Uncle Teo took a huge wrench
and whacked the machine. It coughed and
shivered. SPUTTER, GROAN, EEK!

The machine suddenly stopped. It
leaned to one side. Then it tilted the other
way and collapsed.

Getting Ready

"The machine was fun while it worked," said Uncle Teo.

"Yeah," said Gabi. "But even if you fix it, it won't help me win the bubble gum-blowing contest."

"Why didn't you say bubble *gum?* I have just the thing for you." Uncle Teo opened a drawer and took out a small box. "Inside this box is something very special — Cerebrito's Miracle Bubble Gum! There's only one piece, so take good care of it."

"What's so special about it?" Gabi asked.

"Wait until Saturday and you'll see," Uncle Teo said, smiling slyly. "In the meantime, read the instructions and practice working your jaw up and down."

Gabi thanked Uncle Teo and left.

He tried to read the instructions, but the ink was smeared. He remembered to work his jaw, though, and hoped for the best.

Gabi went over to his friend Pepita's house.

"What's wrong with your jaw?" Pepita asked.

"Nothing," Gabi said. "I'm just practicing for the bubble-blowing contest. Look what my Uncle Teo gave me."

"What is it?" Pepita asked.

"Some kind of special gum. I hope it helps me win the contest."

They could hardly wait for Saturday to come.

The World's Biggest Bubble

Finally the big day arrived. Gabi and Pepita went together to Lincoln Park.

The contest started. The first contestant was a red-haired boy who blew a medium-sized bubble.

Next, a blond girl blew a three-part bubble that split up the middle.

The third contestant lost a tooth inside his bubble.

Then it was Joselito's turn. He took a
breath and blew. A bubble slowly began
to form. At first it looked like a ripe
apple. Moments later it grew to the size
of a grapefruit. Soon it was as large as
a balloon.

But Joselito wasn't satisfied. He kept blowing until his face turned purple. He blew and he blew until . . . POP! SPLAT! The bubble burst. Bubble gum stuck to Joselito's face, covering his nose and cheeks and eyebrows.

Gabi laughed. Then everyone else
started to laugh when they saw Gabi, still
working his jaw up and down.

The judge signaled for Gabi to begin.
Gabi took one last look at the smudged
instructions, crossed his fingers, and put
the gum in his mouth. After chewing it
thoroughly, he began to blow.

A bubble the size of a golf ball slowly appeared. In no time it was as big as a baseball. Then something strange happened. To Gabi's amazement, the bubble began to blow itself! It swelled to the size of a basketball.

"Wow!" cried Pepita.

Everyone stared at the biggest bubble
in the world. They waited for it to burst.
But it continued to grow. It became twice
as big as a basketball. Then three times
as big!

How big would it get?

High in the Sky

As everyone was wondering how big the bubble could possibly get, Gabi suddenly floated off the ground, lifted up by the giant bubble.

"Grab him!" the Mayor yelled. "Pull him down."

But Gabi slipped through their hands and rose above the crowd.

"Spit out the gum!" Pepita shouted.

"I thant," Gabi said, trying to say "I can't." The gum was stuck to his mouth. "I'm thrying to thpit it out, but I thant."

Gabi was ten feet off the ground. A wind lifted him twenty feet in the air. He kept rising higher and higher.

"Watch out for that tree!" Pepita
yelled.

Gabi missed the tree by an inch. He
floated over the park. *How will I ever
get down?* he thought. The park looked
smaller and smaller to him.

The wind carried Gabi past the park and over the town. He gazed down at the rooftops. There was his own house right below!

Then he saw Cerebrito Manor. If only Uncle Teo could help him. "Theo Therabrido!" Gabi cried. But he was too high to be heard.

A flock of pigeons came flying up
behind him. They were heading straight
for the giant bubble. Gabi was afraid they
would get stuck in it. But the pigeons
flew around him at the last second. And
Gabi continued to float high in the sky.

Oh, My Aching Jaw!

Suddenly Gabi heard a great roar.
The air shook. Gabi shook. He looked
up and saw a helicopter whirling above
him. Gabi waved for help, but the pilot
didn't see him. *What am I going to do?*
he wondered.

Gabi closed his eyes for a moment.
When he opened them, Uncle Teo was
beside him. How could that be?

I must be dreaming, Gabi thought.
Then he realized his uncle was standing
inside a bubble. But what was he
wearing? It was a funny-looking outfit
with a pack strapped to his back.

Uncle Teo's mouth was moving
furiously. He seemed to be shouting
something. But Gabi couldn't hear him.

Then, to Gabi's great surprise, Uncle Teo reached out through the bubble, and the bubble lifted away. "Hold on, my boy!" Uncle Teo shouted as he grabbed Gabi around the waist.

POP! Gabi's bubble suddenly burst. Gabi and Uncle Teo tumbled through the air, plunging toward the ground.

Swoosh! The pack on Uncle Teo's back opened into a great big umbrella. No, it was a parachute! They floated down over the park and landed right at the Mayor's feet.

The crowd cheered.

"Cerebrito, you're a genius," said the Mayor. "And a hero, too. What a daring rescue mission!"

The president of The Gooey Chewy Bubble Gum Company gave Gabi a case of bubble gum. "This is your prize for blowing the biggest bubble," he declared.

"Thank you," Gabi said. "But I won't be able to chew for a week. My jaw hurts!"

Everyone laughed.

Gabi shared the gum with all his friends, even Joselito, who looked a little shorter after the contest.

Just then Uncle Teo took something from his pocket. "I found some more of Cerebrito's Miracle Bubble Gum," he announced.

"No more Miracle Gum for me!" said Gabi. "But maybe Joselito would like it," he added, a gleam in his eye.